MODERN
BLOCK PRINTED
TEXTILES

Frontispiece Block-printed velvet by Mariano Fortuny, Venice, *c*.1910

Endpapers "Cherry Orchard" by Paul Nash, printed by Cresta Silks Ltd, *c*.1931

Cover "Welwyn Garden City" by Doris Gregg, printed by Footprints, 1926

THE DECORATIVE ARTS LIBRARY

PARVA·SED·APTA

MODERN BLOCK PRINTED TEXTILES

By

Alan Powers

WALKER BOOKS

LONDON

To Enid Marx

Series Editors
Mirabel Cecil and Rosemary Hill

Tie designed and
printed by Raoul Dufy
at La Petite Usine,
Paris, in 1911.

First published 1992 by Walker Books Ltd
87 Vauxhall Walk, London SE11 5HJ

Text © 1992 Alan Powers

Printed and bound in Hong Kong by
South China Printing Co. (1988) Ltd

British Library Cataloguing in Publication Data
A catalogue record for this book is available
from the British Library.
ISBN 0-7445-1891-1

-Contents-

-Introduction-

Block printing is one of the oldest-known methods of transferring designs and patterns onto cloth. A patterned surface is covered with ink or dye and pressed onto fabric. The pattern, or block, is repeated until the material is covered; several colours may be used. It is a more complex version of the process practised by schoolchildren making lino cuts or potato cuts, and essentially the same as the letterpress process by which nearly all printing was done until the mid-twentieth century.

In fabric printing there is a choice

Scenes from a block printer's life: Susan Bosence draws inspiration for her textile designs from the colours and textures of Devon, and uses natural dyes such as indigo. The sewn resist (below) is an alternative to block printing. The material is bunched up like tie-dye to leave white areas. The pieces on the right use combinations of block printing and dyeing.

between using dyes which penetrate the fibres all through and pigments bound in a medium which tend to stay on the surface. Dyes require more complex handling, for the cloth must be treated with a mordant (usually a metallic salt) in order for the dyes to remain fast. After dyeing, it must be steamed, washed and rinsed several times to fix each colour. Whether dyes or pigments are used, the major part of the work is in the preparation and finishing of the cloth, rather than actually applying a design.

Printing blocks cut
by Enid Marx in the
1920s and 1930s,
using hardwood or
lino mounted on wood,
sometimes with metal
pins for dots.
The block must be
strong but light enough
for easy handling.
Some of these blocks
can be matched to
patterns on pages
40–43.

Even so, block printing is a relatively easy way of patterning cloth compared with weaving a pattern or embroidering it. As a method of printing it was superseded in the nineteenth century by faster mechanical methods, notably roller printing, which helped the English cotton manufacturers to spread their products all over the world from the 1820s onwards. Roller printing uses the same principle of relief printing on a machine, with copper rollers, but the scale of the repeat is limited to the diameter of the roller. It was not only to overcome this that block printing survived as a specialized activity: in addition, it offers a chance for the printer to collaborate with the designer in exercising judgement over every inch of the fabric. The initial investment in producing a design is much less than with roller printing, allowing for greater experiment.

During the nineteenth century, both the production methods and the changing tastes of the public, manipulated through fashion, altered the character of textiles. Aniline dyes, "one of the most marvellous and most useless of the inventions of modern chemistry", as William Morris called them, made available "a series of hideous colours, crude, livid and cheap."[1] Morris reacted against these in the 1860s by reviving traditional vegetable dyes for his tapestries and block prints.

How does a block-printed fabric differ from a machine print? "Designs produced by this method have great liveliness, owing to the tiny irregularities which are inevitable in any hand process," as the design writer Grace Lovat Fraser explained in 1948, "that is not to say that registration is inaccurate in hand block printing. A good block printer can perform miracles of accurate placing in the most intricate designs. But still there is that indefinable quality which always accompanies anything skilfully produced by hand."[2] In other words, the difference comes in enhanced vitality and personality, not by being an archaic mess of badly joined repeats.

Block printing in the twentieth century encompasses the regular textile trade, usually in the reproduction of historic designs by the authentic technique for a specialized market. Between the wars, in Britain, smaller firms could commission their own modern designs and remain independent of the mass-market textile trade, as Tom Heron did with Cresta Silks. At the other end of the scale is the individual craftsman carrying out the whole process from design through production to selling. Block printing requires relatively little equipment or investment, and has the attraction of complete independence. The brilliant designer has sometimes turned entrepreneur and master of a considerable workshop, like Mariano Fortuny, who not only made designs but researched and experimented with all the production processes to achieve new effects. Some designers, such as Raoul Dufy, gained firsthand experience of block printing as a prelude to having their designs printed professionally, with the result that they understood the process intimately.

Block printing as a craft seems to have been a predominantly English interest, although in the Depression years in America it was even used for relieving unemployment. It has played a valuable part in training textile designers and in children's education, but the products of the best craftsmen from the interwar period are gradually being recognized as classics in their own right. As

the clay and glazes are formative factors in pottery, the discipline of block printing by hand creates its own style. Other techniques for applying colour to textiles, such as freehand painting and batik, do not impose such a discipline on the designer. The problems of conservation mean that these fabrics are not often displayed in museums, and the opportunity to handle them is even rarer. This is unfortunate, as seeing them and touching them is the best way to understand their special qualities.

At the end of the 1930s, the simpler and quicker method of hand printing by silk screen swept the commercial field. For craft designers it shortened the time needed for printing, and offered a new and enticing range of design possibilities. As a result, block printing has, regrettably, fallen out of general use in the postwar period.

William Morris

Millions of people who first heard the name of William Morris in the 1960s and 1970s associated it with tightly packed floral cottons produced in a variety of colourways with the name of Sanderson printed along the edge. The modern reproductions of Morris's textile designs are faithful to the original patterns, but, unlike his wallpapers, are screen printed rather than block printed and often far removed from the intensity and delicacy of the original colours.

Although Morris died in 1896, his return to traditional printing and dyeing methods for textiles make him a precursor of the twentieth-century block printers. Morris was seeking better alternatives to the chemical dyes and industrial roller-printing methods which had displaced older techniques. While contemporary

"Brother Rabbit" chintz by William Morris, 1883. An example of indigo discharge with two tones of blue created by repeated dyeing.

designers, like Christopher Dresser and Owen Jones, were content merely to reform the design aspect of textiles, Morris sought also to reconstruct earlier methods of production. He was fortunate in finding Thomas Wardle, a manufacturer from Leek, Staffordshire, who remembered traditional methods from his boyhood. Wardle helped Morris to research and practise various techniques in the 1870s, before he set up his own workshops. Morris had been involved with the production of embroidered textiles, tapestries and carpets for some years; finding the dyeing which he contracted out was always unsatisfactory, he made his own experiments, and became particularly fascinated by indigo.

Indigo is one of the most historic dyes, made from the root of plants grown from India through the Middle East to Africa. It requires experienced handling and preparation, being fermented in a vat at boiling temperature, but gives a rich range of blues. As Morris's biographer J. W. Mackail wrote, "This very uncertainty and delicacy gave it to Morris an additional touch of fascination beyond that of the madder or weld vats. About this time, his hands were habitually and unwashably blue, and in no condition to do fine work."[3] Morris himself wrote that "though this seems an easy process, the setting of the blue-vat is a ticklish job, and requires, I should say, more experience than any other dyeing process."[4]

Patterns can be produced in indigo through batik (freehand

"Strawberry Thief" chintz by William Morris. A slightly faded sample (left) reveals the quality of Morris's indigo and madder dyeing. The main pattern is produced by indigo discharge, with other colours added. The thorough penetration of the indigo can be seen on the back of the sample (below).

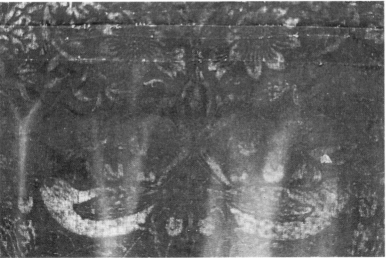

application of hot wax to resist the dye) or by tie-dyeing in various degrees of sophistication. In block printing, indigo is used with the discharge method. It is not the indigo which is applied to the block, but a resistant substance, so that although the whole piece of cloth is immersed in the dye vat, the pattern is washed out afterwards (discharged), leaving white where the printing was applied. The cloth can then be overprinted with other colours.

Indigo discharge was the basis for most of Morris's printed cloths, sometimes in blue and white only, for curtain linings and chintzes like "Eyebright" and "Brother Rabbit", among his most charming and least-known fabrics. More often, the indigo dyeing was the first stage of a build-up of other colours. Morris revived the historic method of making green with an overlay of yellow on blue. The natural dyes fade gradually and beautifully, always giving the impression that the design is integral with the cloth, not just applied to the surface.

Although Morris's designs influenced the whole of advanced English taste and the Morris works produced fabrics for A. H. Mackmurdo's Century Guild, the next generation of design reformers, C. F. A. Voysey, M. H. Baillie-Scott, Walter Crane and Lindsey P. Butterfield, were content to design on paper and leave production to the high-class trade firms rather than get their hands in the dye vat. If one can speak of a first and second Arts and Crafts Movement, with a break around 1910, the first period ignored Morris's initiative and showed no interest in block printing as a craft technique: the focus of textile activity, particularly among women, was embroidery. In the second period, embroidery was less popular and block printing began to take its place, together with hand weaving, both requiring more equipment and professional commitment. When Phyllis Barron made her first experiments in block printing in London around 1911, she was working without reference to William Morris, against whose work she retained a lifelong prejudice. Some of her experiments were, none the less, the same as he had made forty years before and Morris and Co. went on working with his methods at Merton Abbey until 1940.

-The Age of the Ballets Russes-

Wiener Werkstätte

The revival of artistic crafts in Austria before 1914 was centred on the activities of the Wiener Werkstätte, a group of designers and craftsmen brought together in 1903 for the display and sale of work. While the furniture and decorations of Josef Hoffmann and Kolo Moser are well known, the Werkstätte textile designs are less often seen. In fact, the Wiener Werkstätte produced a large number of hand-printed materials from 1905 onwards, mostly silks for dresses, and in 1910 a fashion workshop was also established. This was the year when the Parisian couturier

Brightly coloured designs, like sophisticated versions of folk art, from the Wiener Werkstätte

Other Wiener Werkstätte designs show the bold, almost abstract use of flat shapes and strong colours which became widely influential. The Wiener Werkstätte produced hundreds of patterns for furnishing and dress in the period before 1914.

Paul Poiret visited Vienna and was greatly impressed by their designs.

The Wiener Werkstätte fabrics are closely designed patterns of flowers or geometric motifs with a graphic elegance drawing on folk art and architectural motifs. As repeating patterns their structure is relatively simple. Eventually, their "house style" shared with Dufy and Poiret an interest in the late eighteenth century, elegantly reinterpreted, which was adopted with enthusiasm in England between the wars.

Some of the early designs seem to have been a form of silk screen, but others resemble block prints in technique. With the establishment of Wiener Werkstätte shops in other cities, the influence of these fabrics would have travelled rapidly across Europe, awakening interest in modern design.

Fortuny

The Spanish-born painter Mariano Fortuny settled in Venice in 1889, at the age of eighteen. Fortuny was a precocious but never very successful painter. He was also fascinated by theatrical design. His family had collected antique textiles for many years, and he made an easy transition from designing stage costumes to making printed fabrics for sale.

With the production of the "Knossos" silk scarf and the famous pleated "Delphos" dresses in 1906, Fortuny imitated, as he thought, the styles of ancient Greece which had been popularized by Victorian painters in the Aesthetic Movement, and yet produced something modern and timeless. The theatrical

Mariano Fortuny, dressed in djellabah and turban, in old age.

element in his work coincided not only with the innovative Greek dancing of Isadora Duncan, for which the Delphos was well adapted, but with the revival of the decorative arts all over Europe. Fortuny's interest in textiles included the rich velvets and brocades of the late Middle Ages and Renaissance, extending even to Islamic and Polynesian motifs. All of these he reproduced by printing and dyeing, although they were mostly woven patterns in origin.

Block printing was only one of the techniques used, for Fortuny also patented a machine for an early form of rotary silkscreen printing. Many of the designs included hand painting, particularly of metallic silver and gold. He researched his own dyes, returning to many of the traditional vegetable dyes, including indigo.

Fortuny's earliest designs were block printed by himself, and he personally made all the technical experiments. Eventually he set up a large printing workshop in an upper floor of the Palazzo Orfei in Venice, the main floor of which remains furnished as Fortuny left it and is open to the public as the Museo Fortuny.

Fortuny's fabrics were used for dress and for furnishing. He worked on silks, cottons and velvets, all carefully selected from different parts of the world. As we shall see, it is not unusual for painters to design textiles, but only Fortuny seems to have carried through the whole sequence of design and printing of fabrics, designing clothes and marketing them. These clothes made a strong impression on Marcel Proust, who refers on numerous occasions to Fortuny dresses in *A la Recherche du Temps Perdu*, and

Henriette Fortuny, Mariano's wife, in their workshop at the Palazzo Orfei, Venice.

helps us to imagine the effect that they must have had when new. Proust made the connection with the theatre that ran all through Fortuny's work. The fabrics were not sham antiques but "like the theatrical designs of Sert, Bakst and Benois, who at that moment were re-creating in the Russian ballet the most cherished periods of art with the aid of works of art impregnated with their spirit and yet original, these Fortuny gowns, faithfully antique but markedly original, brought before the eye like a stage decor, and with an even greater evocative power ... that Venice saturated with oriental splendour where they would have been worn and of which they constituted, even more than a relic in the shrine of St Mark, evocative as they were of the sunlight and the surrounding turbans, the fragmented, mysterious and complementary colour."[5]

As Proust recorded, Fortuny's dresses, although utterly unlike the mainstream of contemporary fashion and imbued with an exotic personal vision, were eagerly sought after by fashionable women all over the world. Others could satisfy

Fortuny fabrics seen as rich but simple dresses, revolutionary in their time.

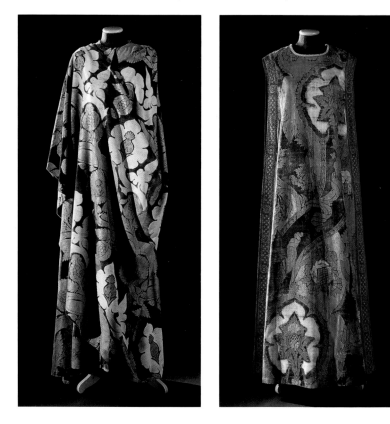

their curiosity in the windows of Fortuny's shops in Venice, Paris, London and New York. His factory on the Giudecca in Venice was taken over after his death in 1948 by the dynamic American-born Countess Elsie Lee Gozzi, who had been involved in marketing Fortuny's designs in New York before the war, and who continues to produce some of the simpler block prints on cotton, although his own magical richness is lost.

Fortuny's painter's eye produced beautiful and subtle combinations of colour, based on historical examples from all over the world.

Dufy and Poiret

The immensely fertile period immediately before the First World War saw not only the launch of Fortuny, but the beginning of the remarkable collaboration between the painter Raoul Dufy and the couturier Paul Poiret. Dufy's textile designs have only recently begun to be appreciated as part of his whole output as an artist. In 1911, when he produced his first fabrics, he was known as an avant-garde painter and member of the Fauve movement, but he had also executed wood engravings for Apollinaire's poems in *La Bestiaire*, deriving in part from the traditional French *imageries populaires*, which formed the basis of his first textiles. These folk-art woodcuts were roughly coloured with stencils, so that the colours did not fit neatly on the outline, an effect that Dufy was to exploit in his paintings as well as his fabrics.

Poiret returned from a triumphant tour of Europe and, stimulated by the fabrics he had seen in Vienna, was then working towards the summit of his fashionable career, giving such extravagant costume parties as *La Mille et Deuxième Nuit*, for which Dufy's first fabrics were created. During the year 1911, Dufy cut blocks and experimented with colours. As Poiret recalled: "We dreamt of sumptuous curtains and dresses decorated in the style of Botticelli. With no regard for personal sacrifice I gave Dufy, who was just starting out in life, the means to realize one of his dreams. Within a few weeks we were setting up a printing studio in a little place in the Avenue de Clichy I'd rented for the purpose. We discovered a chemist called Zifferlin, as gloomy as a winter Sunday, but who had expert knowledge of colourants, lithographic inks, aniline dyes, batik techniques and fixing solutions. There we were, Dufy and I, like Bouvard and Pecuchet, pioneers in a new field which was going to bring new joys and exultations."[6]

The style of these new designs was clearly affected by another of Poiret's experiments, l'Ecole Martine, where girls of about twelve "were made free to do as they liked ... and rediscovered all the spontaneity and freshness of their natures".[7] While impressed by the Viennese designs, Poiret had deplored the restrictive teaching methods practised there and in Berlin –

The "Regatta" dress, 1925, is made of silk printed by Bianchini-Férier to Dufy's design.

"An iron corset to cast their pupils in a new mould" – and wished to demonstrate an alternative. Maison Martine, the decorating firm which was an extension of the Ecole, had a shop in London in the 1920s at No. 15 Baker Street, bringing its influence directly to England.

Dufy made his own versions of the pictorial toiles de Jouy of the eighteenth century using the chunky character of the woodblock rather than the fine copper engraving of the originals. He also designed a variety of floral and abstract patterns in which his painter's eye made the best use of colour, particularly black. After the closure of Poiret's Petite Usine, Dufy transferred his designs to the firm of Bianchini-Férier in Lyons. Some of his designs from around 1919 are astonishing precursors of the Op Art of the 1960s. Dufy designed some elegant painted wall hangings for Poiret's exhibition barges at the Paris Exhibition of 1925, but gave up textile design altogether in 1933.

The panache of Paul Poiret's clothes combined with a bold Dufy pattern in the cape, "La Perse", 1911. His design, "Les Pêcheurs", charmingly brings up to date the French tradition of pictorial toiles de Jouy.

Raymond Duncan

Among the stranger manifestations of the revival of primitive cultures in the early twentieth century was the Akademie Duncan, the school for Greek Arts and Crafts founded in 1911 in Paris by Raymond Duncan (1874–1966), the brother of Isadora. Activities included ancient Greek drama, dance movement, weaving and natural dyeing. Members of the school lived in a vegetarian colony in the suburb of Neuilly, and could reputedly be seen in ancient Greek dress driving their flock of goats along the streets. Later they moved to premises in the Rue de Seine, where the school survived for some years after Duncan's death.

Duncan's speciality was brush-dyed fabrics, including "crepon" hangings and silk pieces for wear as tunics or capes. The larger motifs were painted freehand, but smaller details were block printed with vegetable dyes.

-The Revival of English Block Printing-

Omega Workshops

English artistic life in the years before the First World War was helped out of its conservative isolation by the two Post-Impressionist exhibitions organized by the painter and critic Roger Fry in 1910 and 1912. By showing the work of Cézanne, Matisse and Picasso, Fry promoted the alliance of art and design. Paintings came to be considered as formal relationships of colour and design, not as narratives, and at the same time the Continental experiments in applied art offered an alternative to the rather tired Arts and Crafts aesthetic in Britain. As a practical demonstration of the close relationship between painting and the decorative arts, Fry founded the Omega Workshops in 1912, a loose cooperative of artists and designers; it became the centre of avant-garde design in Britain in the immediate pre-1914 period.

A Victorian sofa, once belonging to Roger Fry, upholstered in Omega fabric.

A swatch of the Omega printed linens of 1913, each 10x15in/25.4 by 38.1cm.

Although textiles were a minor activity, Omega produced some remarkable printed linens, designed by Fry and Vanessa Bell and manufactured in France, probably by Maromme of Rouen, although Fry kept the production details secret. He announced that "a French firm of printers have employed a number of special technical processes in order to preserve as far as possible the freedom and spontaneity of the original drawing."[8] The loose placing of the colours suggests that the process may have involved stencils, although block printing is more likely, using a combination of line and colour not unlike Dufy's. These, though only available for a few brief years, were among the most successful of the Omega products.

Phyllis Barron, the leader of the block-printing revival in England (above) and her partner, Dorothy Larcher (far right). They were recognized as leading craftswomen of the 1920s and 1930s.

Barron and Larcher

Among the artists associated with the Omega Workshops, but not wholly approving of its slapdash methods and disregard of traditional techniques, was a young painter, Phyllis Barron (1890–1964), who had already started her own experiments in block printing. On a sketching course in Normandy in 1905 her tutor, the painter Fred Mayor, bought some old printing blocks for her in a junk shop. She originally thought they were meant for paper, but realizing that they were, in fact, textile printing blocks, she started trying to use them, and found herself embarked upon her life's work.

Barron was unable to get any technical information from the Slade School, where she was then studying, but read what textbooks were available in the British Museum and researched the history of dyes in the Patent Office. She discovered by accident, through the observation of the etcher Thérèse Lessore, that nitric acid splashed on a French blue apron would leave white

Barron and Larcher's Hampstead workshop in the mid-1920s (left). A finished piece of "Flag" fabric is being raised or lowered into a vat. Notice the blocks hanging on the wall.

spots. This was, of course, an indigo apron, and further exper-iments, some of them hilariously disastrous, led to Barron's learning the technique of indigo dyeing, and making her own improvised equipment from gas rings and dustbins. This was followed by her rediscovery of iron-rust dye (a warm black on mordanted cloth, otherwise actual rust colour), and the warm brown vegetable dye, cutch. An instinctive taste, inspired by her painter's training and a knowledge of French peasant textiles, led her to pursue this narrow but rewarding path of delicate natural dyes, rather than using modern dyes and pigments that would have been less troublesome. She chose unbleached linens and cottons which suited her bold designs in these subtle colours.

After her early experiments, Phyllis Barron's colours and shapes became more harmonious. Her interest in natural dyes precluded the use of harsh colours, although she retained the sense of abstract design and pattern which the Vorticists had introduced into their art. She seems quickly to have mastered the cutting of blocks, each a convenient size for the hand to hold. Whereas some block printers cover the face of the block with a fine layer of wool, known as flocking, to make the print firm and even, Barron preferred the rather dry, starved-looking surface produced when an unflocked block is charged with the critical amount of dye paste.

Having worked briefly with Frances Woollard, who later set up on her own, Barron was joined in 1923 by another painter, Dorothy Larcher (1884–1952). The competitive and secret nature of the textile trade made it hard for outsiders to obtain information, but certain manufacturers were generous with assistance and their knowledge of vegetable dyes owed much to the pioneering work of the weaver Ethel Mairet. Even with a limited palette, an enormous variety was possible, and they would sometimes overprint blocks with different patterns as a way of rescuing defective pieces, making a rich complex effect. Although they were famous for muted colours, Barron and Larcher came in their later years to enjoy using brighter combinations, such as a strong red made of pure alizarin (extract of madder) and, later, German chrome colours, as did Ethel Mairet. Apart from rough linens and furnishing cottons, Barron and Larcher worked on finer materials for use in dress, including fine silk and cotton velvets of a quality simply not obtainable now. Dorothy Elmhirst, the joint creator of Dartington Hall in Devon, wore dresses made from Barron and Larcher

Barron's early "Log" pattern, 1915 (top left), overprinted blocks (lower left), "Diamond" galled iron print (below).

fabrics, but they were always a minority "artistic" taste and never aspired to the fashionable heights of Poiret.

Barron and Larcher began to employ a number of girls to carry out printing and other tasks. In a different category was Enid Marx, who joined the workshop as an apprentice in 1925. She describes how she was "broken in" to the long and laborious processes involved: "I worked with them for about a year, printing my own things once a week, but the rest of the time I was virtually their washing machine, rinsing cloth. Luckily Larcher was very keen on washing the cotton velveteen, which had to be taken through a bath of chalk at the end of the process. You can imagine the fun of getting the chalk out of velvet. I started the job, she finished it. It took at least three hours' rinsing with a hose in the garden."[9]

Enid Marx arrived just in time for a large commission to produce fabrics for the Duke of Westminster's yacht, *The Flying Cloud*, whose interior had been designed by the architect Detmar Blow. It was a rush job, and Enid Marx recalls: "We stayed up all night and cooked sausages to keep us going – the Duke was about to set sail."[10] A contemporary of the architect Sir Edwin Lutyens and a specialist in restoration, Blow gave much encouragement to Barron and Larcher in the 1920s, using their fabrics in his own house, Hilles at Painswick in Gloucestershire. There is an interesting transition from the historical revivalism of Blow to the modern design with which Barron and Larcher were associated in the 1930s. The character of their designs did not change, but they managed to produce work of such quality and integrity that it responded to both contexts.

In the 1920s Barron and Larcher's work was already being noticed enthusiastically in the press, while at the Arts and Crafts exhibitions, it contrasted refreshingly with the lingering pre-Raphaelite aesthetic. It was also exhibited and sold by a few specialist London craft galleries, like the Three Shields Gallery in Kensington Church Street and the Little Gallery in Ellis Street, where it would have been seen in conjunction with pots by Bernard Leach and Michael Cardew and other examples of the best modern crafts of the time. They also regularly exhibited

Scraps, mostly printed from old blocks in Phyllis Barron's collection.

at the craft fairs organized by the Red Rose Guild in Manchester.

Barron and Larcher fabrics are simple and seldom in more than two colours. The patterns are either geometric or floral, and both partners could design equally in either style. Many have a strong architectural feeling, which made them suitable for commissions like the Senior Combination Room of Girton College, Cambridge, or the choir stalls of Winchester Cathedral. The colours are mostly within the range of natural dyes that Barron discovered in her early years, including weld and iron in combination which when discharged gave a greenish yellow, and quercitron, for a softer warm yellow.

Barron and Larcher were secretive about their recipes and Enid Marx remembers rushing home to write them down from memory. In 1930, they transferred their workshop from London to Painswick, where they built a fine indigo vat and continued to produce and exhibit until the outbreak of war in 1939, when, in common with most other block printers, they found it impossible to obtain fabric on which to work. Barron never resumed printing, although she helped a younger novice printer, Susan Bosence, to launch her career.

Enid Marx

Enid Marx (b.1902) came to work with Barron and Larcher in 1925, having been failed for the diploma in painting at the Royal College of Art because her work was considered too abstract. As well as studying at the college, then run on rather strict academic lines, she attended the private school run by Leon Underwood, where Henry Moore also studied, which became a centre for the more independent and rebellious students. The Royal College students' magazine, *Gallimaufry*, of 1925, included her in its "Hall of Fame", because "among all the misses who flirt with Art she alone woos it seriously; because she is the Cassandra who prophesies the doom of the old regime of design". This was perhaps a rather over-dramatic prophecy, but in a long career as a designer she has worked in a huge number of fields and enlivened the appearance of everyday objects from postage stamps to formica laminates. Paul Nash, who then taught at the Royal College in the Design School, recognized her skill as a pattern designer and introduced her to the Curwen Press which issued several decorative papers derived from her wood engravings from 1925 onwards. This skill in pattern making was transferred to textiles after Marx had been taken to see Barron and Larcher's work at the Three Shields Gallery.

After her year's training with Barron and Larcher she set up her own workshop in Hampstead, where production continued almost single-handed until 1939. Some of Marx's designs have a family likeness to Barron and Larcher's, since she accepted the same limitations of colour with enthusiasm, and found her work in demand from a similar clientele, but each of the three had favourite styles and periods which acted as sources of inspiration. Barron retained a strong feeling for French traditional design, while Larcher was influenced by years she had spent in India copying the cave paintings of Ajanta and teaching embroidery in an Indian art class. The fact that all three women designers were originally painters and continued to paint and observe nature with a painter's eye is important, as they were not creating patterns in the isolation of a workshop or studio. Fortuny

Enid Marx in her studio, 1988

"Sea", 1928, Enid
Marx, galled iron print
on linen, influenced by
Paul Nash. The
patchy printing was
a deliberate effect,
only possible in
block printing.

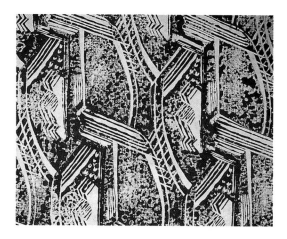

"Wangle", 1932, two-
colour print on dyed
cotton ground. The
boldness reflects Marx's
study of
ethnic textiles.

"Underground", 1933,
iron-rust print on linen.
This was commissioned
by Christian Barman,
who later recommended
Enid Marx as designer
for the seating of the
London Underground.

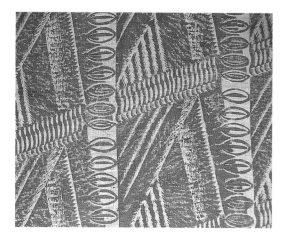

Galled iron print on velvet, showing Marx's skill in constructing a pattern using rotations of the same block.

An alternative combination of the background block of "Wangle" with an overprinted black star

"Woolworth", c.1930, printed with a rubber mat from Woolworths, using tin discharge on cotton dyed in galled iron.

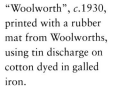

"Cornucopia" (left) and "Basket" 1937 (right), pictorial patterns with a Victorian flavour.

and Dufy were painters too, making clear the interdependency of fine art and design.

Most of Enid Marx's designs are purely abstract, with subtly organized pattern repeats, sometimes involving rotations of the block, with the pattern unit alternately upside down. Of these, some are very simple, with widely spaced stars or dots, and were printed on light dress materials like organdie or balloon cotton left over from First World War production. The dots and stars are never quite regularly spaced, nor repeated with quite the same intensity, giving the whole design a sparkle and humour. It is clear that it has grown under the eye and hand of its own creator, rather than being laid out on a grid by a machine.

In the furnishing trade in the 1920s angular jazz patterns, executed in shrill or murky colours, were becoming popular. Enid Marx's designs are distinguished from this commercial Art Deco not only by their purity of colour and line but by the search for new ways of pattern making, bringing into play a wide variety of sources. "I haunted the British Museum's Primitive Gallery," she recalls (that is, the Ethnographical collection now shown in the Museum of Mankind), where she was particularly inspired by bark cloths from Africa, Polynesia and New Zealand, made from hammered tree bark and often printed with delicate designs in subtle colours. Some designs were inspired by Persian pottery in the Victoria and Albert Museum, and still others by her taste for early Victorian "popular art". The resulting patterns are always fresh and lively. Some were achieved using "found objects" like Woolworths rubber mats instead of engraved blocks, mixing craft and machine aesthetics together.

By the mid-1930s Enid Marx was becoming well known as an all-round designer and illustrator. Her skill in pattern-making was employed by London Transport in the design of seating material for Underground trains. Paul Nash and Marion Dorn, two other designers associated with block printing, were given the same commission, as part of London Transport's outstanding design record in the 1930s. During the war Enid Marx was textile adviser to the Utility Furniture Committee and was in no way hampered by the shortage of colours available for woven stuffs, being used to a limited palette as a block printer. From the small-scale operation of block printing came the experience and inspiration to influence industrial mass production.

Enid Marx pattern samples (clockwise) "Jeux", "Foot", "Chip" and "Richardson".

Paul Nash

Much of the interest in pattern design in the 1920s can be traced to Claud Lovat Fraser (1890–1921), a brilliant graphic artist and designer who specialized in a primitive version of eighteenth-century motifs, clearly influenced by the Wiener Werkstätte which set up an English limited company in 1912. Some of Fraser's textile designs were manufactured for William Foxton, whose enterprising company was founded in 1903.

The painter Paul Nash (1889–1946), already mentioned, became a close friend of Lovat Fraser towards the end of his short life, at a time when Fraser was inspired to design repeating patterns after being given an Italian notebook bound in pattern paper. Fraser's patterns were developed and published posthumously by the Curwen Press in the series of decorative papers to which Nash and Enid Marx contributed. Nash's earliest textile designs date from the same period, around 1920, by which time he was already famous as a painter. The openness and abstraction of "Wild Cherry" suggests that Nash had not forgotten the textiles of the Omega Workshops, with which he had been associated around 1913. Other Nash designs show his experience of abstracting motifs from nature and transforming them into repeating patterns.

When three of Nash's designs for textiles were exhibited in 1921 manufacturers rejected them as not "futuristic" enough. The Omega Workshops manufacturers had mistakenly assumed that modern design meant angularity and brashness, an idea to which Nash's strong but subtle patterns did not conform. "Cherry Orchard" was one of several Nash designs to be printed by the Footprints Workshop, although he was dissatisfied with the quality, and his designs were later contracted out to the trade printers G. and P. Baker before being transferred to Cresta Silks. Nash was very demanding and perfectionist about printing and even marketing. He objected to a Cresta Silks advertisement stating that the firm employed "designers like Paul Nash" on the grounds that there were no designers like Paul Nash, and he insisted that customers in Cresta shops should always be told when they were looking at a Paul Nash design.

DESIGNS FROM "MODERN TEXTILES," 46, BEAUCHAMP PLACE, LONDON. (*Left and right*) LINENS DESIGNED AND PRINTED BY FRANCES WOOLLARD AND ENID MARX RESPECTIVELY; (*centre*) BATIK ON LINEN BY MARION DORN; (*in front*) COTTON DESIGNED BY PAUL NASH AND PRINTED BY "FOOTPRINTS"

Original colour plate from *The Studio Yearbook of Decorative Art*, 1927, showing Paul Nash cotton "Big Abstract" in two colours, printed by Footprints. The design, based on his work as a painter, resembles an abstracted still-life, or landscape.

Footprints and Modern Textiles

The origins of Footprints also involve Claud Lovat Fraser through the workshop his widow, Grace, established in Fitzroy Street as Fraser Trevelyan and Wilkinson. It specialized in theatrical costumes of the kind Lovat Fraser had designed for *The Beggar's Opera* and *As You Like It* at the Lyric Theatre, Hammersmith – productions whose freshening influence on taste in the 1920s can hardly be over-emphasized. Grace Lovat Fraser had appeared as a singer in some of the Lyric shows, such as *La Serva Padrona*, and was to continue as an influential decorator and design journalist into the 1970s. For the costumes small runs of block printing or stencilling were often undertaken.

Among the workforce at Fraser Trevelyan and Wilkinson were Gwen Pike, who had trained at Birmingham, where the Arts and Crafts flourished long after the 1890s, and Elspeth Little, trained at the Central School, where there was also a strong printing and engraving tradition, and subsequently at the Slade School.

Some independent work by Gwen Pike and Elspeth Little was spotted at a charity pageant by Celandine Kennington, the wealthy second wife of the painter and sculptor Eric Kennington. She was inspired to set up the Footprints workshop at Durham Wharf, Hammersmith, in 1925, so called because many of the blocks were printed by foot pressure.

Footprints turned out to be the longest-lasting block printing enterprise of the 1920s. A number of designers were employed, including Doris Gregg, who designed the tightly composed pattern "Welwyn Garden City", more a modernist vision of urbanism than the rambling planning of the actual place. After Mrs Kennington withdrew in 1933 Footprints continued to flourish under the direction of Joyce Clissold (1905–1982), who joined the workshop in 1927 and revived it in a limited form after the war. At its height Footprints had two London shops at fashionable addresses and produced many playful pictorial designs using a much wider range of colours than Barron and Larcher, although without much subtlety of technique. The printing of some later Footprints pieces is of poor quality, but this was compensated by the liveliness of Joyce Clissold's

An atypical Footprints design of sailing boats, 1920s (top left); sample Footprints pattern showing workshop activity (far left below); Festival of Britain commemoration scarf, 1951, Joyce Clissold (left).

Footprints
billhead, 1930s.

designs, sometimes shaped to fit particular clothes or domestic objects, like tea cosies, which she sold from stalls at agricultural shows up and down the country when not pursuing her alternative occupation as a Punch and Judy "professor" on the beach in summer. She also developed a good line in commemorative scarves, sometimes with blocks which could be adapted to different occasions.

When Elspeth Little left Footprints in 1926 she opened a shop, Modern Textiles, in Beauchamp Place, which was one of the small group of outlets not only for textiles but for pottery and other crafts. Paul Nash was a supporter, and designed a signboard and a letter-heading engraved on wood. The shop acted as an outlet both for Footprints fabrics and for other textiles, including early batiks and block prints by the American-born Marion Dorn, better known as a designer of carpets and woven patterns. For printed fabrics Dorn preferred silk screen from its earliest days, as it suited her large-scale motifs. Modern Textiles also became the main agent for the charming and unconventional wallpapers designed by Edward Bawden and printed in sheets at the Curwen Press.

Elspeth Little continued to work as a designer and printer and also became a successful entrepreneur, supplying fashionable decorators like Syrie Maugham. Modern Textiles, well represented at international exhibitions in the late 1920s, helped to increase awareness not only of block printing as a technique, but of a whole look in design and craft of which it formed an integral part. As with Barron and Larcher, this look is particularly fascinating for the way it made the transition from the historic or rustic "period" taste prevalent in the 1920s to the non-period modern movement of the 1930s without any sudden leap.

The Nicholsons

Nash and Lovat Fraser's inspiration can in turn be traced in many respects to the remarkable taste of the Nicholson family – the painter William Nicholson and his wife, Mabel Pryde. William was a dandy who spent his first substantial earnings on a black polka-dot dressing gown and would only paint wearing white cotton duck trousers. The Nicholsons' houses, in Mecklenburgh Square, London (c.1905–1910), and at Rottingdean, used such colours as cobalt blue, scarlet, black and a buff colour described as "the colour of meershaum" in a creative response to the eighteenth century. The style can be found in Nicholson's famous illustrated books, such as *An Alphabet* (1898), and was to influence a whole generation.

With such a background it is not surprising that each of the Nicholson children became in some way involved in interior design. Nancy Nicholson (1899–1977) was briefly married to the poet Robert Graves and tried running a village shop in Boar's Hill near Oxford but was a good illustrator, in a manner close to her father's, and in 1929 found her vocation in setting up Poulk Prints, partly as a jobbing printers and partly for textile printing.

Nancy Nicholson's printed textiles, among the most charming of the interwar period, are quite unlike the usual repeat patterns. She combined block printing with stencilling to create a rich effect of colour, setting a single motif against a patterned backgound in designs like "Duck", "Unicorn" and "Bunch". These were stock designs, and Unicorns hung in several houses designed by her brother, the architect Kit Nicholson, while Ducks continued to be printed intermittently for the rest of her lifetime. Her production was small in quantity and seems to have been largely for friends (except for a period in the 1940s when she ran a shop for Poulk Prints in Motcomb Street, Belgravia), but she designed complete interiors for the novelist Richard Hughes at Laugharne Castle in the 1930s and for the Provost's Lodgings at Oriel College, Oxford, in 1947.

Ben Nicholson (1894–1982), already a rising star of British abstract painting in the 1930s, cut some lino blocks for fabric

"Bunch" block print and stencil by Nancy Nicholson, 1932, commissioned as a child's bedspread.

"Unicorn" block print and stencil by Nancy Nicholson, early 1930s, designed as a bedspread or hanging.

"Numbers", Ben Nicholson, block print, 1933 (above); the contrasting stripe is a device similar to Nicholson's abstract paintings of the 1930s. "Princess" (below), c.1933, at Kettle's Yard, Cambridge; the hanging shows subtle irregularities in the alternation of two blocks.

printing in 1933 at the start of his relationship with the sculptor Barbara Hepworth. They are among the most austere of block prints from the interwar period, being mostly in black, with red stripes in some cases, and a mixture of motifs – letters and numbers, profiles and designs from playing cards. A design like "Spots in a Square" has a strong resemblance to some of Enid Marx's work, but the design "Princess" on two blocks gives most consideration to the effect of a repeated pattern.

Ben Nicholson visited Enid Marx in her workshop to investigate printing techniques, but found them too slow and technical. Instead, he relied on his sister Nancy to print his designs. Nine of his prints were available from Poulk Prints before and after the war, but if it had been Nicholson's intention to earn some additional income, he must have been disappointed, as

very few lengths seem to have been produced. Other Ben Nicholson designs were produced as woven patterns or machine prints by Edinburgh Weavers in the late 1930s.

Kit Nicholson, the third of the family, was an architect whose wife, always known as E. Q. Nicholson (b.1908), was also a painter. Inspired by Marion Dorn to paint fabrics and work in batik, E. Q. printed from lino blocks after 1936, working later with her sister-in-law in the Poulk Prints shop. Her block prints were often direct prototypes for commercial silk screen.

"Black Goose" designed by E. Q. Nicholson, lino block on cotton, 1938; a prototype for screen printing by Edinburgh Weavers.

Silks for Dresses – Crysède and Cresta

Alec Walker (1889–1964) was trained as a painter, like many of the other block printers of the twentieth century, but came from a textile-producing family in Yorkshire. In 1912 his father gave him a small mill from which he began to produce "Vigil Silks". Printed with spots, checks and stripes, these were refreshingly colourful and simple for the time. An answer to his advertisement for a designer for posters put him in touch with the Newlyn colony of artists in Cornwall, where Kathleen Earle, who responded to the advertisement, had studied at the art school. Walker visited many times before they were married in 1918, moving to Newlyn to set up a new firm, "Crysède", in 1920 for the production of printed silks and dresses.

In 1923 Walker was introduced to Dufy in Paris and asked him to make designs for his firm; having looked at Walker's paintings, Dufy said he should design himself. Perhaps more than any other painter-designer of the time, Walker worked directly from observation into abstract pattern. The influence of Dufy is apparent in the bright colours and holiday feeling of the designs, which matched the mood of the 1920s. He was the only designer involved, and the printing was carried out by an experienced team of men. Compared with the work of Barron and Larcher, the Crysède designs used a greater number of colours, normally three or four, but sometimes as many as seven, and a looser, more painterly graphic quality. The blocks were flocked to produce a solid, even colour. Modern synthetic dyes and pigments were used to create bright and vivid effects, but were carefully tested for light-fastness. The fabrics used were mostly crêpe de Chine and georgette silk, although heavy linen was popular for beachwear.

In 1925 Walker was joined by Tom Heron, who had both a textile background, in Leeds, and an interest in contemporary art. Heron advised expanding the firm, and a new building was taken in the Cornish fishing town of St Ives. Crysède already had a number of retail shops in different parts of England, and also sold successfully by mail order. In 1929, a nervous break-down led Alec Walker to withdraw from involvement, but not

Fitting a "Crysède" evening gown, St Ives, 1927. The pattern is "Entracte" by Alec Walker. Draped on the chair is a sample of "Zennor" and hanging on the right, "Isles of Scilly". The titles reflect Alec Walker's inspiration in landscape painting.

before dismissing Tom Heron. The firm of Crysède continued until voluntary liquidation in 1941.

The Wall Street Crash made 1929 an unpropitious year for starting in business, but Tom Heron set up his own firm, Cresta Silks, establishing himself in Welwyn Garden City, one of the idealistic new settlements to the north of London. Like Crysède, the new firm concentrated on the production of block-printed silks for dresses, with contemporary painters as designers. Of these, Paul Nash was perhaps the most famous and Cedric Morris the most prolific. Cresta opened a chain of shops, among the first works of the modernist architect Wells Coates, and the stationery and labels were by E. McKnight Kauffer, the best graphic designer working in Britain at the time.

Cresta designs are similar to those of Crysède, tending towards small-scale patterns in pinks, reds, warm yellows and soft blues, some pictorial and some abstract. Much of Cresta's success lay in identifying a clientele between couture and mass-market appropriate for the hard times of the early 1930s. The purity of the silks made them suitable for wear in hot climates where cheap silks disintegrated. Each shop kept customers' measurements for making up new models from catalogues.

Heron combined socialist principles with commercial realism. His democratic management methods helped to promote the company's identity. After the war silk screen took over for the famous series of silk scarves designed by artists, among them his son, the painter Patrick Heron. In 1947 Tom Heron, already using St Ives as one of his centres of operation, bought up the surviving assets of Crysède and put some of Walker's designs back into production.

Cedric Morris was one of the artists employed by Cresta who also worked for a new textile company founded by the painter Allan Walton in 1930. Walton's textiles were all for furnishing, and pioneered the use of silk screen for printing, giving greater freedom to inexperienced designers. Duncan Grant and Vanessa Bell's later designs were produced by Allan Walton, although never in such quantities as they were by Laura Ashley in the 1980s after the rediscovery of Bloomsbury decorative arts and the restoration of Charleston Farmhouse, their home in Sussex.

Other notable painters, such as the New Zealand artist Frances Hodgkins and even Francis Bacon, were involved in fabric design between the wars. Among those associated with block printing was John Tunnard (1900–1971), who started his career as a design student at the Royal College of Art, and worked for four years in the 1920s for the large Manchester cotton firm Tootal Broadhurst Lee, and then as a carpet designer before moving to Cornwall in 1929 to paint, becoming a popular abstract artist after the war. To improve his income, he and his wife ran a hand-printed silk business from a fisherman's loft in Cadgwith, near St Ives, where Tunnard also formed the fishermen into a jazz band.

Cresta Silks logo by
E. McKnight Kauffer
(above).

"Salukis" or "Myrtle
Cottage Garden"
c.1928, by Alec Walker,
block printed on silk,
showing Walker's
home in Cornwall
and his dog.

Another Cryséde design
by Walker (right).

-Education and Design Reform-

London Art Schools

As interest in block printing grew, several art schools established textile courses in the 1920s and 1930s. At the Royal College of Art the designer Reco Capey, chiefly famous for packaging designs for Yardley, set up a new textiles department as part of the Design School in 1924. Margaret Simeon, one of the early students, recalls it as under-equipped, having only one very dirty sink. Nikolaus Pevsner confirmed "the equipment scanty and hardly suitable for instruction in industrial methods" but the spirit of the classes "cheerful and adventurous". [11]

Margaret Simeon's fellow students used almost entirely black or brown, presumably in imitation of Barron and Larcher's iron-rust prints, but in her diploma show in 1932 Margaret electrified the college by exhibiting brightly coloured floral designs, mostly large-scale patterns loosely based on eighteenth-century motifs, after which black and brown went out of fashion. Margaret Simeon sold some of these designs to Allan Walton, and as a designer went on to work almost entirely for the silk-screen process, much better suited to her large-scale patterns.

Capey, himself the designer of a few block prints, insisted that designs must be tried out on cloth to get the feel of folds in the pattern and the three-dimensional nature of cloth as compared with a design on paper. To the Swedish student Astrid Sampe he said, "Never be afraid to experiment" – advice which she took to heart in reviving the textile industry in Sweden. She still remembers him as "a superb teacher".

At the Central School of Art and Craft, fabric printing was taught by the painter Bernard Adeney, who, although not a practising block printer, was an encouraging and sympathetic teacher and had been associated with Roger Fry before the First World War. He also designed fabrics for Allan Walton.

Block print by Reco Capey, the versatile designer who taught textile printing at the Royal College of Art in the 1920s and 1930s.

Block Printing in Schools

Block printing was also introduced into schools under the influence of the reforming teacher Marion Richardson, who, while working in Dudley, a depressed area of the West Midlands, developed children's art away from Victorian copying towards imaginative design. She used very simple media for pattern making, such as potato cuts, but through an exhibition in Manchester in the 1920s had some of her pupils' designs adopted for commercial production. As she later wrote, "that summer the children could write off to some of the London stores and buy stuff for their cotton frocks which they had themselves designed." It may have been a short-lived fashion, but Marion Richardson did once have the satisfaction of seeing one of the patterns worn by "a very smart lady who jumped out of a taxi one Saturday morning and went into a big jeweller's shop in Bond Street. That pattern, such a spirited one, had been tossed off at ten minutes to four one Friday afternoon by a young rascal who had wasted her time till I threatened not to let her escape unless she produced something reasonable."[12]

Robin Tanner, teaching in Wiltshire in the early 1930s, found his pupils (all boys) needed little encouragement in pattern designing and block printing on paper or cloth after seeing pieces by Barron and Larcher. Tanner later recalled that although it was not possible to print and steam-fix in the professional way, his pupils achieved a good impression without stiffening the cloth, using oil-bound surface inks thinned with turps.

The designs produced in Tanner's class are lively and accomplished. He wrote that "a pattern unit need not always be drawn, it should be made. It is essentially a concrete thing to handle and to use, the effectiveness of the result depending as much upon the arrangement as upon the unit itself."[13]

The number of elementary books on block printing, including Tanner's own leaflet for the "Dryad" series, suggests that it became widespread as a school and amateur craft activity in the 1930s and continued to be popular long after the war.

Block print of boy with a bird by a pupil at Ivy Lane School, Chippenham, Wiltshire, early 1930s, inspired by the teaching of Robin Tanner. Original block (right).

Commercial Block Printing

The growth of modern design in Britain was mainly inspired by examples from the rest of Europe, but the home-grown craft work of the 1920s also raised standards of taste and knowledge. This experience was gradually fed into industrialized production. In a parallel manner, textiles designed with woven patterns were improved by interaction with independent craft designers. Yet even the more adventurous firms were constrained by what their salesmen thought the market wanted, and relied on in-house designers under their direct control, or would only buy designs from freelances with the intention of altering them for their own use. In 1935, W. Turnbull of Turnbull and Stockdale stated that in the trade in general, only three per cent of the designs used came from freelance artists.

W. Foxton Ltd, Sefton and Company, Turnbull and Stockdale and Warner and Sons all produced modern block-printed designs from the early 1920s onwards and their products might be half the price of those from craft workshops – six rather than the twelve shillings a yard for Footprints or Cresta materials. Foxtons was noted as one of the few companies to publicize the names of individual designers, including the architect Charles Rennie Mackintosh, who also sold designs to Seftons in the late years of the First World War. Sadly these were not produced in any quantities and were in any case intended as roller prints, like the striking geometric patterns of Gregory Brown for Foxtons. For designers working on paper, the production method was of lesser concern than for the craft designers.

In the economic conditions of the interwar period, block printing was not prohibitively expensive, in spite of the labour involved. Its main importance came to be for individual artists at the outset of their careers, making the transition from student to professional, for whom it offered the easiest method of small-scale production for sale or as prototypes for mass-production in other techniques.

By the end of the 1930s, taste and style had moved a long way from Phyllis Barron's severe early experiments. A wide range of colours and a mixture of pictorial and abstract designs

were used by design students and commercial studios alike. The quality of the repeating pattern and its suitability for folding and draping continued to be important criteria of judgement, but the more elaborate of the later designs failed in this respect, as well as introducing more colours than were necessary. Growing awareness of the freedom offered by silk screen made the discipline of block printing seem irksome, rather than allowing it to govern the nature of the design.

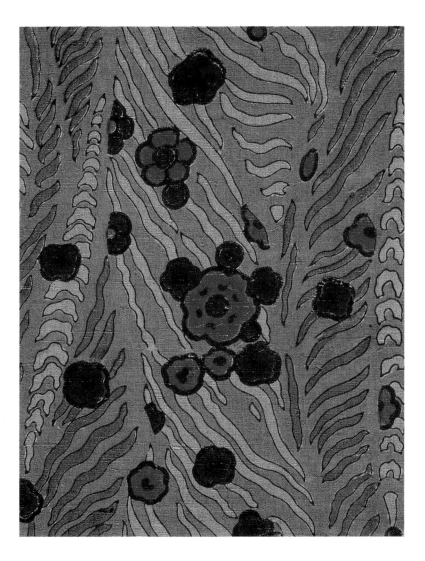

"Cranwell" block-printed linen by unknown French designer *c.*1928, printed by
Warner and Sons, design inspired by Dufy (left).

"Tiger Stripes" designed by George R. Rigby *c.*1918 and printed by
Newman Smith and Newman for Simon and Co. (above).

-From Art Deco to the Depression-

Paris 1925

At the Paris Exhibition of Decorative Arts in 1925 – from which the term Art Deco was later derived – the British Pavilion was not considered one of the best. Indeed, in relation to most of the rest of Europe at this time, British manufacturers had hardly moved forward from the Edwardian period, and the individual artist-craftsmen represented a taste for rustic medievalism which other countries had mostly discarded.

The Scandinavians were much admired in the interwar period for their high standards of modern design, although Sweden, with its strong tradition of textile arts, concentrated on woven patterns and tapestries. Among the block prints at the 1925 exhibition were Greta Jenner's gold and silver prints on velvet and silk and prints in thick pigments on coarse linen by Elsa Flensburg, intended as wall-hangings in the style pioneered by Fortuny. Flensburg also exhibited prints specially laid out for upholstery, made up from a number of small blocks.

Astrid Sampe

Reco Capey's pupil, Astrid Sampe, long acknowledged as the doyenne of Swedish textiles, returned to Sweden from London in the early 1930s and sold block prints through the department store NK (Nordiska Kompaniets). She was commissioned to set up an experimental studio attached to the NK, which was the focus for a revival of Swedish design in printing and weaving, removing the earlier stigma of amateur rusticity attaching to craft work. For the Paris Exhibition of 1937, Sampe presented hand-blocked furnishing fabrics which popularized the Swedish Modern style and was again a major exhibitor at the 1939 New York World's Fair. Another Swedish company, Svensk Tenn, produced large-scale floral designs in strong bright colours by the émigré Viennese architect Josef Frank, in strange contrast to the modernist austerity of his architectural designs.

Block-printed hanging by Astrid Sampe, printed at the Royal College of Art in 1936 under the direction of Reco Capey. The formal experiments of the pattern resemble the work of the Bauhaus. Within a few years, Astrid Sampe was exhibiting block prints internationally.

Indigo print by Marie Gudme Leth, 1935.

Marie Gudme Leth

In Denmark imports from England and Germany had stifled the native textile tradition in the nineteenth century. Marie Gudme Leth (b. 1895) single-handedly revived textile printing, with the aim of improving on the quality of the imported English and German textiles. She had been in Java and seen batik work at close quarters, but her training in textile printing really came from a year at the Kunsthandwerkschule in Frankfurt in 1929. Returning to Denmark, her charming single-colour pictorial designs, printed in indigo and russet, were evidence of a new vitality and as an influential teacher she inspired a revival. It is another story of the individual will and ability of a craft designer having a profound effect on industrial production. Marie Gudme Leth ran Dansk Kattuntrykkeri (Danish Cotton printing workshop) from 1935 to 1940 and her own private studio thereafter, having received a gold medal at the Paris Exhibition of 1937. During the 1940s, she, like Josef Frank, designed large floral patterns, some with direct Indian influence, but later reverted to simpler forms.

Sonia Delaunay

The 1925 exhibition had a strong propagandist purpose in the promotion of traditional French design and manufacturing skills, and therefore carpets and woven silks took their place alongside printed fabrics. Many designers of the time imitated the effect of Dufy's pictorial fabrics, but Sonia Delaunay, who had her own boutique at the exhibition on the Pont Alexandre III, offered an attractive and much-imitated alternative.

Delaunay was herself a painter with an interest in the application of abstract art to dress. Having made a striking effect at the Bal Bullier with the harlequin-like appliqué costumes she had designed for herself and her husband, the painter Robert Delaunay, Sonia received a commission in 1923 from a manufacturer to supply designs, and by the time of the Paris exhibition was well established as a designer of clothes, furnishings, accessories and even geometrically painted car bodies. Her simple coloured geometric designs were block printed in Lyons, and could be worn to striking effect. The patterns could be cut to make particular garments, imposing bold patterns on the human body.

Model wearing coat of Sonia Delaunay fabric (left) with detail of original sample (above).

Details of Sonia
Delaunay's bold and
simple patterns of the
1920s that reflected her
interest in abstract
painting.

Other European Countries

In 1925, the Österreichischer Werkbund and the Wiener Werk-stätte showed printed silks "of a simple character on dark grounds". Fortuny showed fabrics in both the Spanish and Italian pavilions, and in the latter Maria Gallenga Monaci, a Roman designer and patron of the Futurists, showed her stencil-printed velvets and other fabrics which Fortuny considered as imitations of his own.

Most other countries seem not to have shown printed textiles, and none appear to have had the same craft revival in block printing as Britain. In Germany, the woven textiles produced at the Bauhaus were some of its most successful designs, but for some reason no textile printing seems to have been attempted there. In France, Belgium, Holland and Spain batik seems to have been the preferred medium for craft textiles.

By the time of the International Exhibition of the American

Federation of Arts, which in 1931 concentrated on cotton textiles and decorative metalwork, a more detailed picture can be gained of activity in a variety of different countries. France was represented by Sonia Delaunay, Elise Djo-Bourgeois, a noted interior designer of the time, and Pierre Chareau, now better known as the architect of the Maison de Verre in Paris of the same year. As an interior designer, Chareau organized the production of hand block-printed designs by Jean Burkhalter. England, however, produced the largest number of block-printed exhibits, including work by Barron and Larcher, Enid Marx, Marion Dorn, Footprints and Elspeth Little, with commercial prints by Arthur H. Lee of Birkenhead (including designs by Reco Capey) and by Tootal Broadhurst Lee and Co., who commissioned a series of cretonnes from various artists in the toiles de Jouy manner.

The international interest in block printing continued up to the Second World War, and in a few cases beyond. In Switzerland in the 1940s, Carl Eschke of Zurich produced simple and pleasing block prints by Michele Catala, while designers in Finland and other Scandinavian countries continued to work in this medium before the silk-screen revolution overcame them.

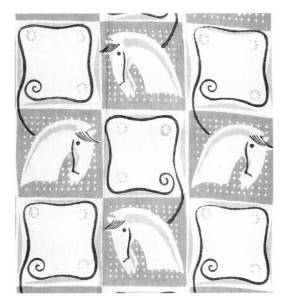

Block print by Lucienne Conradi (Lucienne Day), 1939, printed while studying under Reco Capey at the Royal College of Art. She became one of the best-known pattern designers of the 1950s with "contemporary" prints like "Calyx".

Block Printing in America

The tendency to import textiles from Europe meant that block printing had never become established in America before industrialization and there was little existing basis for a craft revival. In the 1920s craft designers preferred to use batik and the only major American designer of block prints in the early 1930s was Ruth Reeves, who was strongly influenced by her time as a

Ruth Reeves' "Homage to Emily Dickinson", 1930 (left); "Manhattan", 1930 (above).

student in Paris working with Fernand Leger. Although some of her designs have a decorative cubist quality, the main influence seems to have been the pictorial fabrics of Dufy. Ruth Reeves differs from most other block printers in making illustration and narrative her main subject matter, with results that may be deficient as pattern designs but have great charm and period interest. She was exceptional in choosing to illustrate modern life, with the skyscrapers of New York and the home life of the average American family figuring among her subjects.

The patterns were commissioned in 1930 by the firm W & J Sloane of New York, who issued a collection of Ruth Reeves designs and organized the production.

Block Printing in the Depression

During the Depression block printing was one of the activities promoted by the Milwaukee Handicraft Project under the Works Progress Administration, F. D. Roosevelt's imaginative Federal "New Deal" agency. The MHP was intended "to produce by hand such articles of handicrafts which incorporate the basic elements of Art structure", and these included woven and block printed textiles.

The Project began in 1935, receiving, in the words of Elsa Ulbricht, its director, "a motley, careworn and harrassed group of women ... many had been out of employment for so many months that they had become disheartened and depressed... They all had one thing in common, however, the *need* for work, for they were among the thousands of women on relief in Milwaukee County who were crying 'give us work, give us a definite task to do'".[14]

The products varied from simple geometric designs to pictorial patterns with farm animals. As Lisa Richmond writes: "products were often custom designed for specific patrons and tested for suitability. Designer-foremen might take a toy to a schoolroom, for example, or loan curtains to an orphanage, to check reactions and appropriateness."[15]

The WPA also operated an educational block-printing programme in New York, producing results from children of ten or twelve as lively as those by Robin Tanner's pupils in England.

Block prints from the Milwaukee Handicraft Project c.1935. Examples of repeat patterns (above); wall hanging (below) illustrating *The Rubaiyat of Omar Khayam* with excerpts from the poem and six scenes illustrating the text.

-Block Printing After 1945-

The Austerity Years

The outbreak of war in 1939 brought a sudden end to most of the small block-printing workshops in Britain. Supplies of plain fabrics became unavailable, even if the market had still been there. After the war ended in 1945 manufactured fabrics were in short supply, and block printing was found to be a valuable way of recycling old sheets and tablecloths as curtains at a time when the shops had hardly anything to sell. The painter and designer Diana Armfield, who set up with R. H. Passano as Armfield-Passano soon after the war, remembers that "to sustain our business it was necessary to make contact with valuable people in the textile trade who found it possible to get material in ways we didn't ask about". In desperation, they once had to use architects' tracing linen, washing out the heavy dressing.[16]

The London firm of Ascher produced some of the most fashionable printed textiles of the immediate postwar period, including a famous series of silk scarves designed by artists of international standing. These were all screen printed, although in the early 1950s a range of silks was produced using a collection of nineteenth-century blocks discovered by Zika Ascher and adapted with new colourways. A little pattern of roses was made up by Dior and worn by Princess Margaret.

Conditions of postwar shortage kept block printers temporarily in business, but silk screen took over to an increasing extent, both for small workshops and for craft training. Teaching at Camberwell School of Arts and Crafts in the 1950s and 60s, Karin Warming invited visiting lecturers who were printmakers rather than textile artists to inspire the students with the physical quality of relief printing but the fashion for bright colours and large-scale patterns which developed in the 1960s exploited the potential of silk screen, and block printing could not compete.

A few American designs were still block printed after the war

Block prints by Diana Armfield c.1948. Skilful and detailed cutting is complemented by simple single colour printing.

and a rather self-conscious craft revival occurred with the Folly Cove designers. A group of women on the New England coast turned to textile production and supplied block-printed designs for Schumacher in New York, getting themselves written up in *Life* magazine in the process.

Susan Bosence

Phyllis Barron's tradition was carried into the postwar period by Susan Bosence, who, while working at Dartington School in the early 1950s, saw at Dartington Hall some pre-war curtains printed by Barron and Larcher and was inspired to print her own fabrics. Having made a few crude experiments, she visited Barron and Larcher and, apart from being delighted by Barron's personality and discriminating eye, started to learn how to use indigo and the other subtle natural dyes which have formed her style.

Much of Susan Bosence's work is concerned with resist dyeing with wax and sewn resists, rather than with actual block printing, although sometimes these techniques are combined. Her patterns are often derived from effects of light on landscape, or from flowers, but are highly abstract. Their sharpness of outline, often using spots and parallel hatched lines, makes the affinity with Barron and Larcher clear, but even more it is the attention to quality of material and the dyeing process. The colour range is deliberately limited, and grows from a harmony with the Devon countryside with annual visits to the stronger light of southern France.

Susan Bosence's work is known to a few followers of the crafts, but has never been widely exhibited or marketed. Her influence has been spread through her teaching at Camberwell and at West Surrey College of Art and Design, Farnham. Both

Block prints by Folly Cove designers *c.*1946. "Polka Dot Pony" (above) and "Finnish Hop" (left), show lively influence of folk art and popular culture.

schools have been concerned with craft production, as opposed to the more commercial approach of the textile design training given in Manchester. Textile students almost certainly will not continue with these elaborate printing and dyeing methods, but they have the experience and discipline behind them. The publication in 1985 of Susan Bosence's book *Hand Block Printing and Resist Dyeing* made her technical experience and, equally important, her philosophy and approach to working, available to future generations.

Susan Bosence, 1960s to the present, four block prints using simple motifs to best advantage.

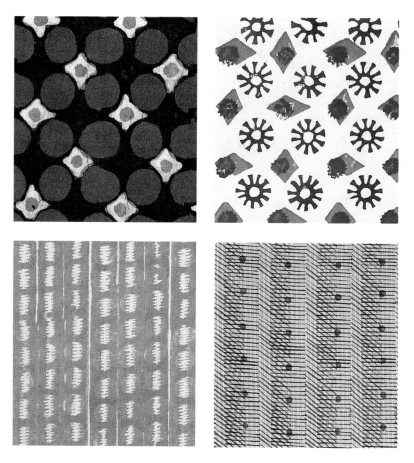

Linda Brassington, block-printed cotton satin with pigment and metallic, resist dyed with indigo.

Linda Brassington – India and Czechoslovakia

Among Susan Bosence's pupils from Farnham is Linda Brassington, now Head of Printed Textiles at the college. In 1989, she was commissioned by the Indian Trade Mission to the EEC to work for three weeks around Jaipur, bringing her design skills to bear on the traditional block-printing crafts of the region. Without imposing her own designs, Brassington persuaded the local craftsmen to use simpler combinations of blocks and subtler colours, re-awakening memories of natural dyes in villages where the excessive use of chemicals had poisoned the only water supplies over recent years. The resulting collection of prototypes is an exciting development, since most Indian block prints are cheaply produced for the mass-market and are little valued. India is the only country in the world where block printing survives as a substantial industry, and the skills of the printers have not been given adequate opportunities.

In 1987, Linda Brassington organized an exhibition of Slovakian indigo textiles at Farnham, including a residency for one of the printers producing these peasant designs with white resist patterns on blue. This particular craft industry has been protected by state support through the communist period. Although its products have yet to find their way onto western markets, it is probably the only continuous survival of a peasant textile printing industry in Europe.

Yateley

Perhaps it is only in exceptional economic circumstances that a block-printing workshop can be kept going in a fully developed country today. Not far from Farnham is Yateley Industries, founded in 1935 by an orthopaedic nurse, Jessie Brown, who had worked in India and thought that the block printing she

Contemporary products
from Yateley Industries.
Child's cotton bag with
"Noah's Ark" block
(right) and detail of
scarf (below).

Blocks at Yately Industries. Those in front have been re-flocked (covered with fine woollen particles), ready for use.

had seen there would provide an opportunity for therapeutic training for the disabled. Yateley produces block-printed articles such as shopping bags, aprons and other clothing to a highly professional standard at very reasonable prices. The working methods favour the production of these as finished items rather than yardage of repeat pattern, although there is a continual demand from decorators for furnishing materials. The designs draw on a large stock of blocks cut from lino and flocked to produce an even printing surface. New patterns are continually added. All members of the workshop are encouraged to make their own designs.

Printing is carried out with pigment colours, with a range of thirty colours mixed from nine dye powders. The colours and designs are deliberately kept in the same style as those of Jessie Brown's period, often reflecting her Indian experiences. The wit of the designs and the bold use of colours recall the work of Joyce Clissold, who was a friend of Yateley over many years. Workshops of this kind are not necessarily well known, and the products are to be discovered in only a few shops.

Norelene of Venice

Visitors to Venice in the last few years may, equally by chance, have seen the shop of Norelene, a fabric printing workshop run by Helène Ferruzzi and her step-daughter Nora. They started researching textile-printing techniques with the aim of continuing the tradition of Fortuny in a modern style, and their work reflects Venice – not so much its own textile history but the

Block-printed velvet by Helène and Nora Ferruzzi ("Norelene") c.1990, evoking the light and textures of Venice.

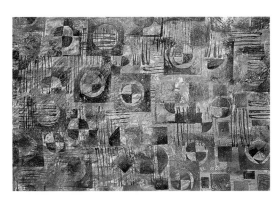

Block-printed silk by Norelene. A typical example of the loose impressionistic build-up of pattern from simple blocks.

Block-printed velvet by Norelene, showing the reflective quality of many overlaid printings, including metallic inks.

effects of light and colour on water which are part of everyday life in the city. The actual blocks used are very simple, and the patterns seldom have regular repeats. Rather, they are composed like paintings, with overlapping accents of colour, often on a dyed ground. The coloured marble pavements of San Marco are one of their inspirations, with the pattern broken up as if seen reflected or through water. In recognition of the presence of gold in San Marco and other Venetian buildings, they use metallic dyes, as Fortuny himself did, on velvet and silk, producing scarves, hangings and dresses. The effect is both rich and simple, exploiting the block-printing technique to avoid the mass-produced and flat look of silk screen, but at the other extreme avoiding the looseness of freely painted fabrics. The work of Norelene is completely contemporary, and offers an inspiration and challenge for other textile designers to discover the possibilities of a neglected and rewarding technique.

-Notes-

1. William Morris, "Textiles", *Arts and Crafts Essays*, 1893, p. 33.

2. Grace Lovat Fraser, *Textiles in Britain*, 1948, p. 142.

3. J. W. Mackail, *The Life of William Morris*, 1899, p. 317.

4. William Morris, "Of Dyeing As an Art", *Arts and Crafts Essays*, 1893, p. 206.

5. Marcel Proust, *The Captive* (translated by C. K. Scott-Moncrieff and Terence Kilmartin, 1983), Part II, Vol. 3, p. 376.

6. Paul Poiret, *My First Fifty Years*, 1931, pp. 160-1.

7. *ibid*. p. 158.

8. Omega Workshops Ltd Artist Decorators, *Descriptive Illustrated Catalogue* (1914), p. 8. Quoted in Judith Collins's *The Omega Workshops*, 1983.

9. "Enid Marx – In Celebration of Her Camden Show", *Designer*, Nov 1979.

10. Letter to author, March 1991.

11. N. Pevsner, *An Inquiry into Industrial Art in England*, 1937, p. 153.

12. Marion Richardson, *Art and the Child*, 1946, p. 35.

13. Robin Tanner, *Children's Work in Block Printing*, 1936, p. 3.

14. Elsa Ulbricht, "The Story of the Milwaukee Handicraft Project", *Design*, February 1944, quoted in *Textiles from the Milwaukee Handicraft Project*, Helen Allen Textile Collection, University of Wisconsin, Madison, 1989.

15. *Textiles from the Milwaukee Handicraft Project*, 1989, p. 3.

16. Diana Armfield, "Design After the War", *A Tonic to the Nation*, ed. Mary Banham and Bevis Hillier, 1976.

Resist print by Lesley Sunderland, 1991. A spirited block print by a textile artist who specializes in hand-painted hangings and furnishings.

-Further Reading-

American Federation of Arts, *Decorative Metalwork and Cotton Textiles*, 1930.

Arts Council of Great Britain, *Raoul Dufy 1877–1953*, 1983.
Thirties – British Art and Design Before the War, 1979.

Hazel Berriman, *Art and Crafts in Newlyn 1890–1930*, Newlyn Orion, 1986.

Linda Brassington, *Modrotlac – Indigo Country Cloths and Artefacts from Czechoslovakia* (catalogue of exhibition at West Surrey College of Art and Design, Farnham, Surrey, 1987).

Susan Bosence, *Hand Block Printing and Resist Dyeing*, 1985.

Sara Bowman, *A Fashion for Extravagance, Art Deco Fabrics and Fashions*, 1985.

Camden Arts Centre, *Enid Marx* (catalogue of retrospective exhibition), 1979.

Reco Capey, *The Printing of Textiles*, 1930.

Hazel Clark, *Textile Printing*, 1985.
"Modern Textiles 1926–1939", *Journal of the Decorative Arts Society*, X, 1986.

Joyce Clissold Textiles, Collages, Drawings 1930–1982 (catalogue of exhibition at Watermans Arts Centre, Brentford), 1982.

Judith Collins, *The Omega Workshops*, 1983.

Jacques Damase, *Sonia Delaunay Fashion and Fabrics*, 1991.

Guillermo De Osma, *Fortuny, Mariano Fortuny: His Life and Work*, 1980.

Department of Overseas Trade (U.K.), *Report on the Present Position and Tendencies of the Industrial Arts As Indicated at the International Exhibition of Modern Decorative and Industrial Arts, Paris, 1925.*

Yvonne Deslandres, *Poiret*, 1987.

Janet Ericson, *Block Printing on Textiles*, New York, 1961.

John Farleigh, *Fifteen Craftsmen on Their Crafts* (includes Margaret Simeon's "Textile Printing"), 1945.

J.W.S. Ferrers, *Fabric Printing*, 1938.

Lillie Fischer, "Astrid Sampe", *Antik & Auktion*, Helsingborg, April 1990.

"Folly Cove Designers" Life, XIX, 26 November 1945, pp. 80–83.

Christopher Frayling (with research by John Physick, Hilary Watson and Bernard Myers), *The Royal College of Art*, 1987.

Marjorie Orpin Gaylard, "Phyllis Barron (1890–1964), Dorothy Larcher (1884–1952); Textile Designers and Block Printers", *Journal of the Decorative Arts Society*, III, 1979, pp. 32–39.

Traude Hansen, *Wiener Werkstätte, Mode, Stoffe, Schmuck, Accessoires*, Munich, 1984.

H.G. Marshall Hayes, *British Textile Designers Today*, 1939.

Patrick Heron, "Tom Heron", *Journal of Decorative Arts Society*, IV, 1980, pp. 34–39.

Hochschule Für Angewandte Kunst, Vienna, *Josef Frank 1885–1967*, 1981.

Hunterian Museum, Glasgow, *Charles Rennie Mackintosh, the Chelsea Years 1915–1923*, 1978.

Brenda King, "Cresta Silks Ltd", *The Textile Society Magazine*, XV, 1991, pp. 4–8.

Susan Lambert, *Paul Nash As Designer*, 1975.

Griselda Lewis (ed.) *Handbook of Crafts* (contains an essay on textile printing by Margaret Simeon), 1960.

Jeremy Lewison, "The Early Prints of Ben Nicholson", *Print Quarterly*, I–II, 1985, pp. 105–124.

Charles Marriott, *British Handicrafts*, 1943.

Valerie Mendes, "Marion Dorn, Textile Designer", *Journal of Decorative Arts Society, II, 1978.*

Paul Nash, "Modern English Textiles", *Artwork*, II, 1926, pp. 80–86.
Room and Book, 1932.
"Modern English Textiles", *Listener*, 27 April 1932, p. 607.

Charlotte Paludan, "Stoftrykkets Gennembrud i Danmark", *Nordisk Funktionalisme 1925–1950*, Nordisk Forum for Formgivningshistorie, 1986.

Dora Perez-Tibi, *Dufy*, 1989.

Nikolaus Pevsner, *An Inquiry into Industrial Art in England*, 1937.

Paul Poiret, *My First Fifty Years*, 1931.

Marion Richardson, *Art and the Child*, 1948.

Stuart Robinson, *A History of Printed Textiles*, 1969.

Stuart and Patricia Robinson, *Fabric Dyeing and Printing*, 1–3 Dryad Leaflets, 1976.

Barley Roscoe, *Hand Block Printed Textiles: Phyllis Barron and Dorothy Larcher*, (exhibition catalogue, Crafts Study Centre, Bath, 1978).

Astrid Sampe-Hultberg and Adolf Grosskopf, *Textiltryck*, I–III, NKI Stockholm, *c*.1950.

Gosta Sandberg, *Indigo Textiles, Technique and History, 1989.*

Mary Schoeser and Celia Rufey, *English and American Textiles from 1790 to the Present*, London, 1989.

Werner J. Schwieger, *Wiener Werkstätte: Design in Vienna 1903–1932*, 1984.

Joyce Storey, *Textile Printing*, 1974.

Robin Tanner, *Children's Work in Block Printing*, 1937.
Double Harness, 1987.

University of Wisconsin, Helen Allen Textile Collection, *Textiles from the Milwaukee Handicraft Project, 1989.*

Josef Vydra, *L'Imprime Indigo dans l'art populaire slovaque*, Prague, 1954.

York City Art Gallery, *The Nicholsons, The Story of Four People and Their Designs*, 1988.

-Places to Visit-

Few museums have permanent displays of block-printed textiles, although they may have examples which are not on show. Some of the collections listed here are open only by appointment, so it is advisable to contact places listed in advance of visiting.

Austria
Östereichisches Museum
für Angewandte Kunst
Vienna

Denmark
Kunstindustrimuseet
(Museum of Applied
Art)
Bredgade 68
1260 Copenhagen K

France
Musée de l'Impression
sur Etoffes (Museum
of Textile Printing)
3 rue des Bonnes-Gens
68100 Mulhouse
Haut-Rhin

Musée des Arts Decoratifs
(Museum of
Decorative Arts)
Palais du Louvre
Pavillon de Marsan
107 rue de Rivoli
75001 Paris
Seine

Great Britain
Crafts Study Centre
Holburne of Menstrie
Museum
Great Pulteney Street
Bath
Avon   BA2 4DB

Royal Cornwall Museum
River Street
Truro
Cornwall   TR1 2SJ

Victoria and Albert
Museum

Cromwell Road
South Kensington
London   SW7 2RL

Warner Archive
Warner Fabrics plc
Bradbourne Drive
Tilbrook
Milton Keynes
MK7 8BE

West Surrey College of
Art and Design
Falkner Road
The Hart
Farnham
Surrey

Whitworth Art Gallery
University of Manchester
Whitworth Park
Oxford Road
Manchester
Greater Manchester
M15 6ER

Yateley Industries
for the Disabled Ltd
Textile Printers
Mill Lane
Yateley
Hampshire

Italy
Museo Fortuny
Palazzo Fortuny
San Marco 3780
Campo San Beneto
30124 Venice

Norelene
San Marco 2606

Campo San Maurizio
Venice

USA
Museum of Fine Arts
465 Huntington Avenue
Boston
Massachusetts   02115

Art Institute of Chicago
Michigan Avenue at
Adams Street
Chicago
Illinois   60603

Helen Allen Textile
Collection
1300 Linden Drive
Madison
Wisconsin   53706

Cooper-Hewitt Museum
The Smithsonian
Institution's National
Museum of Design
2 East 91st Street
New York
New York   10028

Fashion Institute of
Technology
Seventh Avenue at 27th
Street
New York
New York   10001-5992

Goldstein Gallery
University of Minnesota
10 University Drive
Duluth
Minnesota   55812

-Acknowledgements-

I would like to thank my editors for their encouragment and skill in shaping the book. Many museums have answered enquiries and provided illustrations. I would particularly like to thank Barley Roscoe of the Crafts Study Centre, Bath, and Neil Harvey and Paul Harrison of the Victoria and Albert Museum Department of Textiles for arranging study visits to their collections and providing documentation. Other curators who have helped in Britain and abroad are Deborah Abramson and Marianne Carlano (Boston Museum of Fine Arts), Hazel Berriman (Royal Cornwall Museum), Dilys Blum (Philadelphia), Dorothy Bosomworth (Warner Archive, Milton Keynes), Monique Drusson (Musée de l'Impression sur Etoffes, Mulhouse), Lynn Felsher (Fashion Institute of Technology, New York), Beverley Gordon (Helen Allen Textile Collection, University of Wisconsin), Jennifer Harris (Whitworth Art Gallery, Manchester), Susan Mayor (Christie's, London), Dr Sandro Mescola (Museo Fortuny), Charlotte Paludan (Kunstindustrimuseet, Copenhagen) and Richard Slavin (Schumacher Archive, New York).

Among the block printers themselves, I have had much help from Diana Armfield, Susan Bosence, Linda Brassington, Ann Cox (Yateley), Lucienne Day, Enid Marx (who also read the text in draft and made valuable suggestions), Astrid Sampe, Margaret Simeon and Karin Warming. Angela Taunt, Polly Walker and John Watson (Wimbledon Fine Art) have helped in providing illustrations. Other specialists in textile history have been generous with information, notably Brenda King and Margot Coatts.

Tea cosy by Joyce
Clissold of Footprints,
1950s.

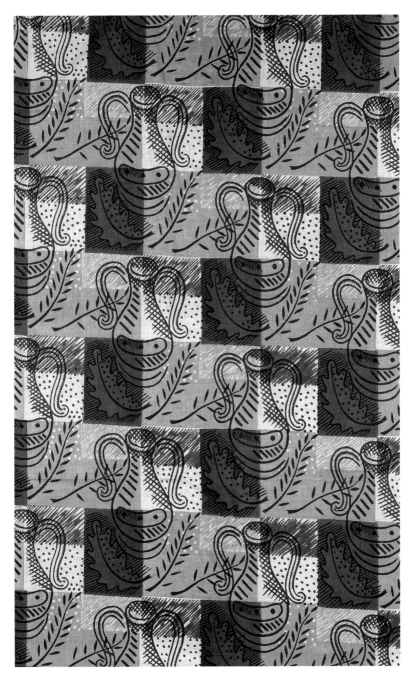

Block print on cotton by Jane Edgar for Gerald Holtum, 1939.

-About the Author-

Alan Powers was born in London in 1955 and studied art history at Cambridge University. Since completing a PhD on Architectural Education 1880–1914, he has worked mainly freelance as an historian and artist. His publications include *The English House* (with Clive Aslet), *Oliver Hill, Architect and Lover of Life* and *Shopfronts*. As a printmaker, he has published individual prints and the sets of prints *Seaside Lithographs*, *The English Tivoli* and *The Marches*.

From 1985 to 1990, Alan Powers and his wife Susanna ran the Judd Street Gallery from the shop which forms part of their home in Bloomsbury; they exhibited many young artists and craftsmen, as well as publishing limited edition prints by Enid Marx, Eric Ravilious and other modern British artists. The publishing side of the business continues. At the same time, Alan Powers has been involved in conservation of twentieth-century buildings, through the work of the Thirties Society, of which he is now Honorary Secretary. He was a lecturer at the First World Congress on Art Deco at Miami Beach, Florida, in 1991, and is organizing a successor Congress in England in 1995. He is Honorary Librarian of the Art Workers Guild and a regular contributor to *Country Life*, *The Spectator* and *Crafts*.

Woodblock by Enid Marx for "Foot"
(see p. 43). Drawing by
Alan Powers

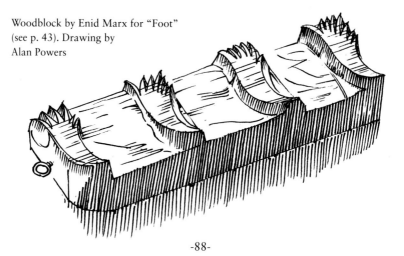

Susan Bosence's studio in Devon, with sample book and tools

-Picture Credits-

Helen Allen Textile Collection,
University of Madison, Wisconsin: p. 72

Diana Armfield: p. 74
(photos Richard Holt)

By courtesy of the Board of Trustees of
the Victoria and Albert Museum:
cover, pp. 47, 48, 57 (lower), 59, 69, 70,
86, 87, 90, 92, 93

Linda Brassington: p. 77

Christie's, London: p. 30

Crafts Council: pp. 10–11, 76–7 (photos
Richard Davies)

Jaques Damase, Paris: p. 67

Anthony d'Offay Gallery, London: p. 31

Flammarion, Paris: pp. 8 (private
collection), 27 (private collection), 28

Holburne Museum and Crafts Study
Centre, Bath: pp. 32, 33, 35, 40
(centre), 41 (centre)

Sally Hunter Fine Art Ltd: p. 42

Kettle's Yard, University of Cambridge:
p. 52 (photo Alan Powers)

Kunstindustrimuseet, Copenhagen:
p. 66 (photo Alan Powers)

Enid Marx: pp. 12, 40 (upper), 40
(centre), 41 (upper), 43 (photos Alan
Powers)

William Morris Gallery, Walthamstow
(Woodmansterne Publications Ltd): p. 14

Musée de l'Impression sur Etoffes,
Mulhouse: pp. 19, 20, 29, 68
(photos G. Barth)

Museo Fortuny, Venice: frontispiece,
pp. 23, 24, 25

Norelene, Venice: pp. 80, 81

Schumacher Archive, New York: p. 75

Lesley Sunderland: p. 82
(photo Alan Powers)

Angela Verren-Taunt: p. 52
(photo Alan Powers)

Polly Walker and the Royal Cornwall
Museum: p. 55

Warner Fabrics plc: pp. 61–2

West Surrey College of Art and Design:
pp. 17, 35 (lower), 37 (photos Alan
Powers)

Whitworth Art Gallery, University
of Manchester: endpapers

Wiltshire County Council Library
and Museum Service: p. 60

Wiveca Siterius, Helsingborg: p. 65

World of Interiors: p. 39
(photo Peter Lavery)

Yateley Industries for the Disabled:
pp. 78, 79 (photos Alan Powers)

York City Art Gallery: pp. 49–50
(courtesy of Annelise Graves), p. 53
(courtesy of Edinburgh Weavers)

Block print of Nairn Cloth, influenced by Joan Mirò and surrealism. Nora Jean
Campbell, 1939.

-The Decorative Arts Library-

Early English Porcelain
Bevis Hillier

Modern Block Printed Textiles
Alan Powers

Point Engraving on Glass
Laurence Whistler

Rag Rugs of England and America
Emma Tennant

Block-printed linen by Anne Morgan and Karin Warming, *c.*1939 (above).

Block-printed rayon by Kate Elizabeth Lyons, *c.*1939 (left).